FLASHLIGHT

EXETER WRITERS

CONTENTS

Introduction

Su Bristow

Wikipedia defines flash fiction as 'a fictional work of extreme brevity that still offers character and plot development'. As you'll see from this collection, however, it can be anything from a story to a kind of snapshot; a prose poem, a play or even a shopping list. The only thing shared by all of these pieces is that they are short.

Flashlight offers you a selection of *amuse-bouches*. Some will give you a momentary taste of sweetness (and sometimes not so sweet), while others will linger in your imagination, hinting at wider possibilities. They are not designed to be consumed all at one go. Dip in, savour a few, and save the rest for later.

Their creators are an equally mixed bag. Exeter Writers range in age over several decades, and some are much-published while others are just starting out. We have poets, playwrights and non-fiction authors among us, and almost every genre is represented. What we have in common is the desire to write well and the willingness to learn. We hope you enjoy our stories!

Su Bristow
Chair, Exeter Writers

You can find out more about our authors on the Exeter Writers website: www.exeterwritersorg.uk.

A Light

Michele Evenstar

I'm on the northbound side of the tracks, facing the sun, what there is left of it. It's the sort of sky that could turn either way: in ten minutes it could be pouring, or I could be standing here dazzled by the last of the sun's rays ricocheting off rails and the platform's damp grey slabs.

My body feels stiff, heavy, but I suddenly want to run, to let motion consume my misery.

I used to run: half-marathons, marathons and, of course, all the training in between. I loved it so I'm not sure why I let it drift away. We do that, don't we? Forget to pay attention to the most important things in our lives; let them disappear, barely noticing as they are carried off on a tide of work and trivial obligations.

In the deepening gloom I can still make out her window from here, just there – the fourth house along from the southbound platform. Funny how all those years commuting on the train I could probably see, for a split second anyway, straight into her bedroom without for one moment thinking that one day I'd be there, under the duvet, holding the woman who lives in that house.

I'm waiting for a light. If it comes on, she's telling me not to get on the train. Then I'll leave the station and wind my way through the little back streets to her home and know that we can leave the past behind, that we can offer our futures to each other.

But it's late; the train will be here in a few minutes and there is no light. I can feel the cold creeping up from my hands and feet. Soon it will meet the chill spreading from my chest.

The rails start to sing, and I see the train emerging from the distance, its bright Cyclops eye glaring fiercely down the length of the rails. It gradually pulls up, brakes screeching painfully. The doors wheeze open and I step up onto the train, glancing back hopelessly at her house.

I wonder if my brain is making it up: tiredness? Desperation? I stand frozen in the gangway, staring, blocking everyone. There is a faint flickering at her window. I look out across St Anne's: no illumination except from a few cars, their headlights burrowing along dark streets, arcing across buildings. There's a power cut…she's put a candle in the window!

I whirl around and push past irritated passengers. I reach the doors as they slam shut. The train creaks into motion. It doesn't matter. I'll run all the way back from the next station.

A New World

Emily Sharma

Kate holds Gary's head just above the water. She knows she'll have to heave him up further. He smells like shit and alcohol and something musky and mean. She manoeuvres her hands under his arms and pulls him up another step, then two, then three, until she can't do any more and she rests, catching her breath.

'Wake up,' she tells him, but he's gone, eyes rolling in boozy oblivion.

She'd felt the flood coming, smelled it in the air, warned Gary. 'Daft,' he'd said, chugging on a can of Stella. When he'd seen water spilling over the sandbags, seeping through the floorboards and out of the toilet, he'd hit the whisky. He was incoherent by the time it was four inches deep in the kitchen and out cold when it rose over the edge of the sofa.

Kate should have been moving the furniture up, saving stuff, rescuing mementos, but she'd stayed in the bedroom staring at the text from Robert.

You all right?

She knew he meant because of the flood, but she kept looking because its existence meant someone cared.

When the fields turned silver she packed a bag, listening to the rain drumming incessantly on the roof. As darkness fell, she sensed the energy change.

Her legs are cold. Gary's body no longer holds any warmth. She wriggles out from under him just as the lights go out.

'Shit,' she says into the darkness and she pulls her phone from her top pocket, turning on the torch. Gary looks dead. His head is flung back against the stair, his legs floppy in the water. For a moment she contemplates pushing him back down, watching him float away into the darkness, but she shuffles back underneath him, her tired arms pulling at his armpits until at last he's out of the water and lying on the landing.

Below her an eerie echo wraps around the house. She's marooned in claustrophobic darkness. Exhausted, she crawls along the landing to the bedroom and slips under her duvet. The cold cracks at her bones. With numb fingers she sends a text. *It's dark. I'm scared.*

When she wakes, Robert is standing beside her bed, grinning in an orange shell jacket.

'C'mon,' he says. 'There's more to get to.'

'You came,' she says. Her head is fuzzy with sleep and she's not sure if she's dreaming.

He smiles and nods towards the open window. 'Boat's outside.'

The curtains flutter in the breeze and Kate rises from the bed and walks towards him. Outside his yellow dinghy bobs just below the sill. The dawn is breaking over a vast silver sea. A new world has arrived overnight. Treetops sit like shrubs in a giant bird bath and houses have been reduced to bungalows, their top windows peeping from the water like exotic sea creatures. The breeze is tangy and fresh; it brings possibility rippling towards her across the grey water.

'Just you then, is it?' Rob says, looking around the room. His eyes are dusky-blue, safe.

'Yes,' she says. 'Just me.'

Robert lowers himself into the boat and reaches out his hand. 'Let's be away then.'

The outboard motor splutters into life and they move away from the house, cutting through the silver water across and out into a new world.

Angel

Emily Sharma

She was sitting on the back step the day she first saw the angel. Cramps squeezed at her belly, so she rocked back and forth trying to ease the pain. Tears flowed freely down her red, chafed cheeks.

It had landed on the step, a single, curled feather with fronds near frozen in the January frost. It rippled in the breeze then rolled to the side, before taking off again and gently floating out over the garden wall.

In that moment she decided that a visitation had been made.

When her blood didn't come the following month and when, at last, she witnessed the exquisite expansion of her belly, she thanked her angel, keeping the knowledge of it secret, as if to talk about it might jinx the luck it brought.

'There's something in your smile,' her husband told her, as they lay slumped and lumped, his arm thrown proprietarily across her. 'As if you hold a secret.'

'Tsh,' she replied, unable to hold his gaze. 'You imagine things.'

Now, in the oppressive heat of an August afternoon, she slowly moves her heavy body to the back door and looks out to the trees, begging the leaves to stir. Hot air claws her skin and her dress grips, vice-like, around her middle.

The angel wends its way towards her in a downward path, zigzagging across the sky on the lightest breath of air. It falls at her feet, nestling against her big toe.

'Hello, my friend,' she says, stooping to pick it up.

A sudden pain grips her, forcing her to her knees. 'Harbinger of change,' she whispers, and smiling she blows the angel from her palm, watching as it floats off to other climes.

Labour comes fast and furious. With no time for her husband to be fetched, she is whisked, siren blaring, through the heat-exhausted streets.

The hospital room is a flurry of concerned faces. Breathe slowly, they coax, don't push – not yet. She groans, surprising, alien sounds.

At last, release, her baby girl bursts from her in a sudden gush as hands bother and fuss. A white blur in towelling, they take her to the side of the room.

She listens and hears nothing but the beating of her heart.

She listens but the room is quiet and grim.

She looks imploringly to the window as the endless seconds drag.

At last she sees her angel. Slowly it drifts down, floating along on a crooked trajectory, to the sill where it rests.

A gasp; a breath of air and a wail. Her daughter bellows her welcome to the world and she too breathes again.

The delivery room doors heave open and heat and masculinity bluster in. Her husband's face, waxen with worry, scans the room. A kindly nurse ushers him forward to greet the mewling bundle.

He walks across the room, his stride nervous, his hesitation beautiful. He peers down at his new-born daughter.

'Hello, Angel,' he says.

Bunny McNulty's Memoranda

Hayley Jones

Church Harvest Supper

Order flowers
Call Rev Phillips re Fiona singing
Organise catering — Molly Keith, Jane Cunningham
& Lorraine Phillips?
Plan menu
Ask Charlie to take photos. Also Beckton Gazette?
Arrange waiters — younger choir members? (NOT
Sean Osmond)
Discuss song choices with Fiona
Find musicians to accompany (Bobby Cunningham
has already agreed to play violin)

To-Do List w/c 2nd September 2019

Laundry
Ask Fiona for afternoon tea on Friday

Vacuum downstairs
Dust/polish downstairs
Bake Victoria sponge (Fri or late Thur)
Clean bathroom
Clean downstairs lavatory

Memorial notice draft
5 years gone but not forgotten
Gareth Alexander McNulty
(6th March 1973 – 28th September 2014)
Beloved son of Kathleen "Bunny" McNulty and the late Arthur McNulty MBE
Fiancé to Miss Fiona Bebbington
Tragically taken while serving the public
(Beckton Gazette charges £25 per line & £40 for decorative border = £195)

To-Do List w/c 9th September 2019
Invite Rev Phillips and Fiona for Lunch — Wednesday?
Place order for memorial notice
Order flowers for Gareth's grave
Laundry
Vacuum downstairs
Vacuum upstairs
Dust/polish everywhere
Clean windows
Clean bathroom and downstairs lavatory
Suggest Reverend Phillips delivers sermon on fidelity in near future

Church Harvest Supper
Order flowers

Find waiters (anybody but Sean Osmond)
Source thank you gifts for Molly Keith, Jane Cunningham & Lorraine Phillips — nice wine? (Might not be wise for Lorraine?)
Source thank you gifts for Fiona and musicians — wine or chocolates? Flowers for Fiona?
Source thank you gifts for waiters — chocolate
Check church hall has enough crockery, cutlery, glassware, etc.

To-Do List w/c 16th September 2019

Ask jewellers in Beckton whether Fiona has sold her engagement ring to them
Write to bishop re inappropriate relationship between Fiona and Rev Phillips
Laundry
Meet with Rev Phillips to confirm harvest supper arrangement

Letter draft — use the good stationery and deliver by hand

Dear Fiona,

I'm sorry to feel obliged to write this missive, but I must express my utter outrage and devastation, disappointment and sadness regarding your recent conduct with Reverend Phillips. Gareth would have wanted you to find love again, but there is no way in hell he would have wanted to see you bring shame upon yourself and his memory by carrying on with a married man, particularly a member of the clergy.

Please refrain from embarrassing yourself, poor Lorraine and my late son.

Yours sincerely,
Bunny (Kathleen) McNulty

Church Harvest Supper
Beg for waiters — offer payment if necessary
Order blackberry wine from Smith's Farm Shop
Buy chocolate in Waitrose /Tesco?
Borrow or rent wine glasses (Lorraine Phillips must have plenty)
Organise music rehearsal — does Rev Phillips need to be present?

To-Do List w/c 23rd September 2019
Invite Fiona for anniversary dinner on Saturday (suppose one ought to, if only for sake of tradition)
Send cheque to Beckton fire station for obstacle race fundraiser — £500?
Vacuum downstairs
Dust/polish downstairs
Clean downstairs lavatory

To-Do List w/c 30th September 2019
Finalise harvest supper arrangements
Collect wine glasses from Lorraine Phillips
Write thank you note to Beckton fire station crew (be sure to mention how proud Gareth would have been)
Phone Beckton Gazette and ascertain whether they are sending a reporter/photographer to the harvest supper on Saturday

To-Do List w/c 7th October 2019

Write letter to Fiona, informing her of my shame, anguish and disappointment

Cut all contact with Fiona from now on

Write to bishop re Rev Phillips's replacement — ask for new vicar to be appointed ASAP

Call on Lorraine Phillips — take flowers (and details of nearest Alcoholics Anonymous meeting)

Buy thank you gift for Sean Osmond (especially kind of him to persuade his friends to be waiters, too) — perhaps gift card for The Amazon so he can get a computer game?

Cut Gareth's memorial notice out of last week's Beckton Gazette and put in blue shoebox.

To-Do List w/c 14th October 2019

Decide what to do with the engagement ring Fiona put through the letterbox — blue shoebox or bury at Gareth's grave?

Carnage

Clare Girvan

'Can't you come off that phone for five minutes?'

'I'm just playing *Go*.'

There's something about destruction that is quite compulsive. Like seeing a chimney stack being blown up, or a dam collapsing.

Or broken crockery, with all its different shapes, patterns and colours, that almost looks like a work of art. Something modern, that says something about contemporary society, our broken laws and unwritten rules.

Our rules, anyway, mine and Ed's. We started breaking the rules years ago. In small ways at first, a tiny insignificant lie here and there, which led on to bigger things. Big lies, big deceptions.

Total honesty was what we promised each other, but once total honesty had been breached by a few small lies, just fibs, really, total deception somehow crept in.

'Do you like this dress?'

'How much was it?'

'Only twenty, reduced.'

The dress had been £40.99, but I knew he would complain if I'd told the truth, even though I had my own account.

'You're late back,'

'Yes, I went to see Mum.'

I'd been having coffee with Lorna who Ed didn't like, so where was the harm in saying I was elsewhere? He did the same, claiming to have only been in the pub for a quick one, or keeping quiet about Janine flirting with him at work. Harmless, and all done with the best of intentions, but once you've got away with it, the next time is easier.

I knew the flirtation with Janine had gone much further. Little things: working late, the shower when he came in, the furtive phone calls – did he really think I hadn't guessed? I would check his phone when he'd gone to bed, obviously. Then there were too many clean shirts, avoiding mentioning Janine's name, using the word 'someone', the sort of thing that wives of straying husbands know all about. It became almost a game, spotting the signs.

Actually, I didn't care all that much. Our 'married life 'had become non-existent; we could go for hours without exchanging a word and I never bothered to laugh at his puerile jokes. There wasn't a lot left. I thought sometimes about having an affair myself, but there hadn't been much on offer and I couldn't really dredge up the energy to try. Years of living with someone like Ed breaks you down.

The thing I hated most was his crosswords. He loved them and would buy little books of them to do in the evening while I watched television, which he despised as a waste of time.

'I suppose you think crosswords are a good use of it?' I said.

'They are. They keep your synapses working and prevent dementia.'

I hoped they would. The thought of nursing Ed through dementia was too awful to contemplate.

'What's a seven-letter word meaning "total bloody destruction"?'

'Armageddon.'

'No. Seven letters.'

'Google it.'

'No, it's not worth anything if you cheat. I'll go down the road and have a think.'

He never asked me to go too, and once the door closed behind him, I picked up his cup and threw it at the wall. Coffee dregs trickled down the wallpaper as china shards settled on the carpet. So I threw his plate as well.

Like lies, once you've started, it's hard to stop. I threw everything that would break, the tea set still intact from our wedding, my cooking bowls, the vases, mugs, teapot, glasses, until the cupboards were empty and the carpet was covered in coloured crockery and glass. In the light from the lamps, it looked quite pretty. I stamped on a few pieces that hadn't broken sufficiently, then went upstairs and packed a bag with my favourite dresses, a few books, underwear and shoes. I left a note on the table for when he came back. It said: *Seven letters: Carnage.*

Changes

Su Bristow

It was three in the morning when the mirror spoke to him. He'd been staring into it for hours, seeking some answer from those dark, shadowed eyes. If you looked for long enough, you started changing into something else. He thought maybe he could hold onto the change, somehow crack open his sixteen-year-old, acne-scarred skin and crawl out, damp and soft, until his wings dried and he could fly free. But it was a bitter winter night; no butterfly could live out there. And all the mirror said to him was, 'Well, that's your life over, then.'

Still, somehow, it went on. Clare grew rounder and more beautiful, and stopped coming to school. His essay on global warming won a prize, a place at the world climate change summit in Boston, in

September. He was there when the call came, two weeks early, edging along a campus path through overgrown shrubbery dripping with autumn mist. He had to leave at once.

There was a journey like a dream, a taxi cab through rain-wet, empty streets, a hospital full of harsh lights and busy people. And then, suddenly, a small room warm with candlelight, and Clare gripping his hands and staring into his eyes. No more changing, now; he was her anchor in the wide, stormy sea. And then, at last, he was aground, holding in his arms his damp and wrinkled daughter, fresh from the ocean, just beginning to dry.

Half-way to Hank

Dianne Bown-Wilson

Harry had known it would be today. For all their prevarication and hope of last-minute rescue, he'd seen the jaws of the beast were wide open and the end was about to come.

Previously he hadn't wanted to alarm her but, sure of what they faced, he'd sat down with his wife the night before and talked about his plans.

'It's now or never,' he said. The comparison verged on disrespectful, but he felt like a soldier leaving for the Front. When he came back home tomorrow, he wouldn't be the same.

'We need to move quickly,' he told her. 'It won't be easy, but it can be done.'

She took his hand, 'I'll start first thing.' She'd stand by her man.

Even for February, the morning is dank, rain more a promise than a threat. In the gloom of daybreak, workers surge through the gates, unknowing automatons starting just another day.

A number of them, the jokers, call out or whistle as they pass. 'Hey, where's your gee-tar, Elvis?'

He grins and good-naturedly gives them the finger, but mainly he just walks on: a red-jacketed, crepe-soled, country boy, rebellious in a sea of black.

Apart from a few who've become his friends, most have never seen this side of him before. He's just one of the suits, the upstairs mob; a research and development techie – not much use to them. It'd never been what he'd wanted, but he'd followed the sensible path. Doing what society expected. Living an industrial factory-farm death.

He gave it his best, almost his all, but it wasn't meant to be.

If his heart is going to be broken, it won't be over this. Parading his true colours, his soul unfettered, he's defiant in meeting the end. When it comes to 'surplus to requirements 'he wants to show them it's a game they both can play.

Two hours later, blank-faced men retrace their steps, subdued as if in the presence of death. Not him. He's sauntering, head held high, invincible as a tank.

Those around him walk like zombies, shaking hands gripping their phones. Already they're scrolling around job sites, texting acquaintances, calling mates to seek advice. Between now and when they pitch up home, they have to figure out what to say. Anything rather than admitting the words: redundant, laid off, on the scrapheap, let go.

Unemployment adopts a range of disguises but, in this town, its bite is the same. Lives filleted of meaning, dignity stripped, hope gutted. The end.

Not Harry. He's made his decision; he and Sarah are heading off. With a demo-tape of country music, his red jacket, and a list of contacts, he's set to follow his dream.

'Hey,' someone calls to him. 'Comin' to drown yer sorrows?'

'No thanks, mate, things to do.' He smiles and walks on. In his head, on a loop, there's an anthem: *I'm going to Graceland. Graceland, Tennessee.*

No longer Harry, he's half-way to Hank; his walk becomes a swagger.

(First published in Writers' Forum*, March 2020)*

Hanging Around

Margaret James

There's no way out of this.

I can't go up.

I can't go down.

I'm stuck.

They're laughing at me, all the other members of the university potholing club, every single one of them a man. They'd never wanted a girl in their gang. So when I messed up spectacularly this morning, they were all delighted.

'Still like it up there?' calls one.

'Course she does! She's the fairy on the Christmas tree,' another jeers.

He has a point.

As I'd abseiled down into the cavern which the club would be exploring later on today, my harness had got caught on an enormous stalagmite. I'm hanging there, my waterproofs all torn, my headlamp smashed, and feeling worse than mortified.

They crack a few more jokes at my expense, and then –

'Must be time for a pint, lads,' says Bob Miller, the group leader. 'We'll get out the easy way this time.'

Off they troop along the passage, leaving me in the pitch black, still dangling.

I won't call after them. I damn well refuse. They'll have to come back for me. They can't leave me in the dark to die!

They do come back. But it's hours later, after I've wet myself and frozen all my bits off.

It's a long slog, a medical degree, but I finally qualified, and nowadays I'm a registrar, specialising in urogenital surgery. There's a new list today and when I see the name, I blink. Robert Miller, booked in first today for a minor but tricky procedure. I'll be assisting the consultant, Mrs Cox, and yes, she's heard all the jokes.

I introduce myself to Bob Miller, who is already looking nervous at the thought of a couple of women interfering with his bits. Pale and twitching, he's clearly anxious to get on with it and get the hell out of this place before he goes to pieces.

'Oh, hey,' I say cheerily. 'Mr Miller – good to see you again. The last time was up in the Lakes, remember? When we were in the potholing club?'

I take his notes from the hovering nurse, scan them, and then I make a few changes to the list. Bob Miller will be last, not first, today – and, since his case is not an emergency, if some of the other procedures take longer than expected, he might have to come back tomorrow.

Or even the next day.

'I'm afraid we're a few hours behind this morning,' I add, smiling. 'So I'm sorry, but you're going to be hanging around here for quite some time.'

Hits

Cathie Hartigan

Dennis didn't want much. Two things, that's all. More hits on his website and for Liam Sadler to stop calling him Penis.

'But Dennis has a d and two n's.'

'Two ends?' Liam nearly wet himself.

Apart from Liam sitting a boot-kick-to-the-chair distance behind him, Year 8 IT was cool. Dennis came top having coded his own website, but following an initial flurry from the nosy, the number of hits had nose-dived. Dennis had asked his mum for the cycle helmet camera thinking it would provide material, except he never saw anything interesting.

Liam had only used a simple template but everyone loved his blog, *Behind the Scenes at the Supermarket*.

'None of it's true.' Liam told a queasy Mr Tomkins, who'd questioned the rat in the fruit store and ants in the bakery.

One day, while cycling past Liam's house, Dennis saw him in the garden with his dad. Something definitely wasn't right, so without being seen he hid behind a car, while making sure his camera had a good view.

Back home he went straight upstairs to watch what he thought he had heard. Yes, that thudding noise had been Mr Sadler hitting Liam. And it hadn't been a little cuff; Liam had actually fallen over. There were words too. Apparently, Liam was a tosser, a total waste of space and much worse.

At Monday break, Dennis clutched a memory stick containing the footage in his pocket. He wondered if it was the same in a shoot-out, sweat slicking the trigger. How many shot themselves in the foot?

'What is it, Penis?' Liam was suddenly there. 'Getting extra smell from you today.'

The plan was to give him the memory stick and say that if he ever called him names again, he'd post it online.

'I...I...' He stared at Liam's forehead, half of which was yellowy-brown. It looked as if Liam had tried to hide it with his fringe. 'I'm sorry about your bruise,' he blurted.

Liam looked at him sharply. 'What's it to you?'

'N...nothing. It looks bad, that's all. I just wanted to ask for...for your...*help*.'

The word plopped into the space between them like the first fat raindrop of a storm.

'Help?'

'Yes, help,' squeaked Dennis, fumbling for the memory stick. Where was it? Had it vaporised? 'Only I was wondering...wondering...' He almost blue-screened, but then, like a miracle, it came to him. 'Seeing how you and me are the only ones who know anything in IT, whether we could, like...'

'Like what?'

'Like, work together?'

'*Together*?'

'I've got an idea, see,' Dennis rushed on, in a mad trolley dash of invention. 'I know my website's crap. Yours is brilliant, the content and everything, but you can't code for toffee.'

Liam shrugged. 'So? What's the big idea?'

'One site. I'll help you with code, and you can help me with content. It'll be, you know,' he drew quotation marks in the air, '*collaborative working*. We'll get millions of hits and Tomkins'll love us.'

Dennis could see by his frown of concentration that Liam was caught. He wondered if it hurt.

'But what would it be about?' said Liam.

'Well, we could do anything. Footie if you like, or climate change.' The bell went for the end of break, and they headed back together. 'I've got a camera on my cycle helmet now,' said Dennis. 'We could be detectives or something.'

Liam gave him a sideways glance. 'You reckon?'

'Yes,' said Dennis, 'like Holmes and Watson. You'd be Sherlock, of course.'

Liam laughed, and Dennis felt such an easing in his chest, he decided to take a risk. 'Maybe we could make it a single-issue site. Bullying's a big thing,' he said, 'and abuse – there's a lot of that about.' He gulped, then added, 'I gather.'

There was a hiccup in Liam's step, and Dennis felt the old anxiety rush back. He had physics next, and Liam wasn't in his group. They'd arrived at the point of separation.

'So?' asked Dennis.

Liam didn't say anything for a long moment, but then: 'Cool. Okay, Dennis. Laters, yeah?'

Dennis watched him go, squeezing his hands into fists and thrusting them deep inside his pockets to stop himself punching the air. The small rip in the lining gave way under this onslaught and the memory stick, lodged between his pocket and his pants, dropped down his trouser leg, tripped over his trainer and clattered onto the path.

He picked it up then slipped it into his other pocket. Later, he'd wipe it clean. Maybe.

In the Light

Jan Cascarini

They stopped beside the old street-lamp to study the music, hemmed in by the tight circle of light.

'Show me where you mean,' he said, fumbling with the pages. She pulled off a glove and, taking it from him, tapped lightly with a finger at the score.

'Just here,' she said, lifting the page closer to the light. 'We'd finished this line before you came in: you were late.'

He rested a hand on hers to steady the paper as they both peered at the dots, their breath forming a brief cloud in the crisp air. She traced her finger further back through the score, then began softly humming the soprano line. He joined in with his part and they sang the harmony quietly together. She'd never realised how thrilling a bass voice was, close to: the vibrations were almost palpable. It took all her self-control not to let her head rest on the source of that deeply seductive sound.

'You know what it was,' he murmured, his lips brushing her ear. 'The tenors were racing away as usual, taking you with them. It wasn't us at all.'

He was looking down at her, their heads close enough for her to feel the warmth of his breath on her cheek. It could happen so easily now, if she let it. They were at the tipping point of intimacy. Should she? Did she want it that much? Temptation and fear mingled as her finger wandered back to the top of the page and she began la-la-ing the melody again, a touch louder than before. Once more his voice joined hers, singing the words this time, almost at full volume. Their heads nodded to the beat, voices swelling with the melody until, reaching the bottom of the page, they both broke off and looked, laughing, at each other. Then suddenly the levity vanished and the question in his eyes was unmistakeable. Her courage fled, but as she turned her head away, her eye was caught by something else, something glinting in the lamplight by her foot. She allowed her attention to be diverted by this… What was it? It looked almost like…

'Good God!' She let go of the score and bent down. 'It's my…it must have come off my finger when I took my glove off!'

Hastily she put the ring back on her finger and pulled her glove over it. 'That's extraordinary!' she whispered, smoothing the black suede.

'Extraordinary,' he said. 'A good thing you looked down.'

She could see disappointment in the way he stood, motionless, regarding her.

'I must go,' she said. 'I'll see you next week.'

'Yes.' He folded the music and tucked it inside his coat. 'Next week.'

Lost and Found

Lottie McKnight

I feel like I'm dying, my legs screaming at me with every step.

It's been hours since I've seen another soul, and I can't help wondering if the event organisers and marshalls have cleared up and gone home? Maybe they collected up the signs too, assuming I'd dropped out halfway around. Was there an obvious turning I'd missed? The path up ahead does look like the road less travelled.

Part of me considers turning around but, having not seen a peep of civilisation since I started, it makes sense to trundle onward. You can't walk that far in England without crossing a road, can you? Maybe if I keep going, I'll reach the sea? Although, even with my limited geographical knowledge, I'm quite sure the Peak District is nowhere near the coast. I'm more likely to stumble into a housing estate.

With only the dappled golds and reds of sunset for guidance, I fight my way through an almost impenetrable wood, knitted and twisted branches stretching out to snag on my clothes.

A twig snaps a hundred yards away. I freeze and glance around, my vision fighting against the ambiguity of dusk. At the hoot of an owl, my legs break into a sprint, darting between fallen trees towards the thinning canopy.

The wood transitions into rugged moorland, stars illuminating the night sky. An old wooden sign stands a few yards ahead, tall and ominous under the dappled moonlight. I reach up to scratch off the lichen growing across the white letters. Peering closer, the words spell out Pennine Way. I was hoping for McDonalds to be honest, or 24hr Tesco; anything but the expanse of mute-grey moorland stretching out towards the warm amber halo of town lights far in the distance.

Without warning, two pinpricks of light appear to my left, then the faint rattle of an engine. My heart lurches – headlights!

My feet stumble along the stony path to the adjoining road, jazz hands waving down the van like an aviation marshall on steroids. The driver swerves and slams on his brakes before winding down his window. 'Jesus, love, I could have hit you!'

'Sorry. Any chance of a lift into town please?' I mutter. My hands shake with part relief and part adrenaline from being mown down.

'Yeah, sure, love, but I've gotta do a job first in the next village.' Written in big bold letters across the side of the van are the words, Rural Electric.

'Thanks.' I slick down my hair and force a smile in an attempt to look normal and less like I've stepped out of a horror movie.

He leans over to open the passenger door and I climb in beside him. 'What yer doing out here so late on your own?'

'I got lost.'

'Where've you come from?' His eyes sparkle with amusement in the moonlight. He's rugged, in a handsome way.

'London.' I say, before realising he means where I started my walk.

'Yeah, you're definitely lost!' He roars with laughter.

We stop for half an hour outside a customer's house and I stay in the car, eyes closed and mouth open, catching moths. A nudge and I snort awake outside my hotel – *The Pennines Inn*, sniggering again at the tacky neon sign with its missing *n* and *e* letters.

'Great name for an inn!' He chuckles. 'Fancy joining me for supper at the pub down the road?'

My stomach growls in response. He hasn't axed me to death on the moorland, so I'm thinking it's a safe bet. 'Yeah, sure. Give me ten minutes to freshen up.'

We spend the evening in the pub laughing and drinking before Keith escorts me back to my hotel. 'Fancy a walk tomorrow?' he teases.

'No way!' I laugh. 'Never again.'

'How about lunch instead?'

Mick Jagger and the Cigarette Butt (A Memoir)

Cherry Gilchrist

'You kept one of Mick Jagger's butts,' she said. 'And a tin of Coke they'd drunk.'

'No – no, not me,' I replied. What a sleazy idea. I had chased the Rolling Stones, I admit, but I wouldn't have stooped to that.

'Oh well, must have been someone else,' Marion conceded graciously. We were old acquaintances, meeting again at a funeral and reminiscing on being teenagers back in 1963.

My friend Helen and I did pick them out, the Rolling Stones, and that's something to be proud of. They were just a supporting band on the bill in Birmingham when we discovered them. But we recognised their talent, befriended them, wrote them dozens of letters, and followed their trail as best we could. Fourteen-year old schoolgirls with watchful parents and little pocket money didn't get too much chance to roam, although it's amazing what we managed. We took trains and buses to places like Coventry and Worcester, and devised ingenious tricks to get in backstage, such as announcing confidently, 'I've been asked to take a message to the band.' (That one did work, occasionally.)

The Stones drove around in an old Commer van, which we learned to recognise half a mile away. They recognised us, too, frenetically waving and ready to be their willing slaves.

'Get us a cup of tea, Cherry,' said Keith Richards in the greasy spoon café, and my world was complete.

At one concert, forbidden to enter backstage, we pushed ourselves up on the window ledge outside, trying to get a glimpse into their dressing room. Inside was a memorable scene – Mick and Charlie were reading a letter from Helen and laughing fit to bust. She had a talent for humour – later, she wrote radio scripts for a living.

Helen and I divided the Stones up between us. She was to have Mick, and I would have Brian Jones. The shaggy blonde hair, the slow sexy smile…It's all there, in my diary, which is covered with embarrassing scrawls: 'Brian! Brian!'

I don't think Brian ever replied to my outpourings, though Bill Wyman did when I asked him to clarify their song lyrics. *It's* "Where's it at?" *not* "Where's my hat?", he wrote back in patient amusement. Such letters and signed records from various Stones were tossed out with scorn in my later teenage years. They would have been worth something now.

But I do have my diaries to check up on all those touching details of our meetings.

Here's one account: *At about 6.30 we saw a van coming and Brian waving to us! Wow! Introduced him to our policeman friend, and Brian sort of backed away nervously.*

I can't think why.

But now I turn back to the entry for that first, life-changing encounter in Birmingham – and what's this? *Mick is quite nice and he gave me a fag to keep and we got some fag ends and souvenirs and things off the others and then we walked down to the hotel with fair-haired Brian and we thought umm yes we like him then we thought…*

The diary is a ruthless reporter. Memory is a fickle thing, our hold on it ephemeral. It charts our journey of passion, even though the feelings inscribed there may be ephemeral too. When Brian died in 1969, the year I turned twenty, I'm afraid I just didn't care anymore.

(*First published on Cherry Gilchrist's blog site*: cherrycache.org, *2020*)

My Wife is Very Creative

Elizabeth Ducie

'My wife is very creative.'

What else can I say? She's obsessed with our dog. We haven't spoken for years, apart from discussing thread colours. If I see one more picture of a cute little poodle, I'm going to strangle her. No, none of these is appropriate. So I trot out the same trite phrase as always: 'My wife is very creative.'

As the potential buyers wander around the house, I look at it through their eyes. The small picture in the hall *is* cute. A chocolate-coloured miniature poodle with a huge stick in its mouth. I remember the day we took it, just after Galaxy arrived to live with us. He found this stick, almost as big as himself, and tried to carry it with him. But it kept getting caught in the hedge in the lane. In the end, he dropped it and stared at us with a puzzled look in his eyes. We both loved that dog then.

As we move into the lounge, the portrait over the fireplace draws our eyes. In charcoal, with just a hint of colour for the eyes and nose, she took months to get it just right. And when it was finished, I framed it for her, as a birthday surprise. The three of us went out for tea in the cafe by the river—the one that welcomes dogs.

The embroidery started a few months later. First it was a small canvas, one I know we will see when the tour continues upstairs; but gradually they grew bigger and most of the walls in here are covered in them. A poodle at rest, a poodle at play, a poodle barking in mock anger. Each one drawn on canvas by hand, and lovingly stitched.

The *pièce de résistance* is the hearthrug, semi-circular, hand-knotted in rich browns and creams, with black eyes and nose. It provides a place for its model to lie in front of the fire every evening when we watch television.

'My wife will be back in a few moments,' I say, to fill the embarrassingly long silence. 'She's just taking the dog for a walk. Why don't we take a look upstairs while we're waiting?' The couple smile and nod, although I suspect, by the look on their faces, we are probably all wasting our time.

As we turn to leave the room, the young woman glances at the only picture in the room not featuring a poodle. A small unframed photo of a blond child in romper suit, laughing up at the camera from his mother's lap.

I know next time I look, the photo will be back in the drawer where my wife hides it; and I will take it out, as I have daily for ten years, and tuck it back into one of the picture frames. And from the look that young woman gives me as she walks out of the room, I believe she knows that too.

Nothing Changes

Cathie Hartigan

My dentist announced that a crown was necessary, and the sooner the better as beneath the old filling there was quite a bit of decay.

'Nothing lasts forever,' he said breezily, as we said goodbye. I was not so cheerful. Expensive news, and further evidence of my physical decline, so instead of going straight home, I set off for some seaside therapy. A walk would be good.

Late September sun, and the sea dazzled. The Holiday Shop dazzled too. Full of bright primary reds, blues and yellow it displayed an array of windbreaks, rows of buckets with proper turrets and matching spades. There was only one customer; a dad in pink Bermuda shorts, helping his small son choose from a large crate of kites.

'This one?' He pulled out one sporting a happy Nemo.

The boy shook his head.

'Look,' said Dad. 'How about Buzz?'

Another shake.

'You can't see them all, Dan. We'll be here forever.'

The kites, most furled like umbrellas, were a bewildering eye-level kaleidoscope for the toddler. Eventually Dad's patience decided the matter, a jolly green dinosaur on a rainbow background, but as they crossed the road and headed down to the beach, the boy looked over his shoulder several times at what might have been. I wasn't in a hurry and stopped to watch the kite released into the stiff breeze. It flapped almost crossly, making a racket like an old-fashioned football rattle, but then, once full, it silently soared. The boy's pure, unadulterated pleasure was more worthy of attention though. He stood still as if a spell had stuck his soles to the sand. Arm out straight as a sentry's, only his head moved this way and then that, as he tracked the kite's flight. I hoped the string tied around his wrist would hold, at least for a while.

It was busy in the vicinity of the shops, mostly with elderly holiday makers. A couple slowly made their way towards me, but it was the bench facing the sea they were after. The man gestured at it, as if warning me off, not in an aggressive way; his concern was clearly for his wife. It was impossible not to notice the swollen state of his wife's legs: blotched and purple, with no delineation of the ankle at all, indeed flesh spilt over the edges of her sandals. Poor woman, I thought, when and how did that happen? Overnight, or over years. It certainly put my tooth decay into perspective.

'There you are, love,' he said to her, as she sat on the bench with a sigh. 'Comfy?'

She smiled up at him. 'Yes, thanks.'

'Ice-cream?'

'In a minute.' She patted the bench beside her. 'You have a sit down first.'

I was nearly past them by this time, but couldn't help noticing the grunt of effort involved in bending his knees. He gave one of them a rub once he'd made it to sitting, but then picked up his wife's hand and together they surveyed the scene.

'Excuse me,' I said, as I interrupted their view for a second.

They both waved away my apology.

I glanced back once I'd passed. There was a tenderness about them that touched me, and I'm glad I did because he was leaning over to give his wife a kiss on her cheek.

'Nothing really changes,' he said. 'Does it, love?'

I leant on the handrail, rendered weak suddenly. Had he said black was white or hot cold? Hardly, but that was how his remark struck me. Teeth, ankles, knees, of course they deteriorate! But intangible, more important things can grow and flourish.

Across the estuary the bright beach at Dawlish Warren, further off the dark cliff of Berry Head on the horizon, jutting out like a ruler laid on a sheet of paper, and then the bank of black cloud: it would soon muscle in. Above me, the kite still flew, a box of paints amongst the drab opportunist gulls. Helped by his dad, the boy had learned to guide it already. Pulling on the string, he ran back and forth along the smooth wet sand, as the kite performed marvellous somersaults high over the sea.

Proposed Amendments to School Rules, in Light of Recent Events

Hayley Jones

(Copies to be made available to all governors, staff and parents.)

1. All non-canine assistance animals require the head teacher's approval on an individual basis.
2. Applications for assistance animal approval must be submitted prior to the start of term.
3. Successful assistance animal candidates, i.e. those deemed appropriate, must be kept under their handler's control AT ALL TIMES.
4. Hygiene procedures for assistance animals

must be agreed in advance and followed consistently. Failure to adhere to hygiene procedures will lead to reconsideration of approval status.

5. If hygiene procedures fail, it is unacceptable to utilise the effects for the purposes of abuse or "comedy".

6. In the event of an assistance animal destroying property belonging to the school, staff or pupils, its handler is responsible for compensating all parties.

7. Pupils and staff are advised to give careful consideration to any personal items they wish to bring onto school grounds. While not banned, the following items are not recommended: hair gel, expensive fountain pens (particularly heirlooms), tablet computers, passports and anything else which might be judged potentially edible by a goat.

8. Pupils are reminded not to pass judgement on other pupils' assistance animal requirements. Any concerns regarding the assistance animal should be discussed with the head teacher, but discussion of disabilities, illnesses, conditions, etc is not permitted.

Note:

Christopher Warren has written an apology, which will be circulated to all pupils, staff, parents and governors. Mr Warren understands the scepticism concerning his son's assistance animal, but since bringing Gerald to school his anxiety symptoms have improved and his attendance has increased by 273%.

In future, Gerald is permitted to stay in a dedicated area on school grounds, but will not be allowed in class. Mr Warren has arranged to replace all destroyed items and issued personal apologies to those affected. As a goodwill gesture, he has replaced Mrs Riley's chair.

Remembrance

Emily Sharma

She's selling poppies on the corner of the High Street. The shock of seeing her sends him reeling and he props himself up against a doorway, out of sight, and reaches for his tobacco. His hands shake as he rolls a smoke.

Standing there in jeans and a woolly jumper, cheeks flushed pink with cold, she seems the same. Perhaps her hair's a little shorter, her frame slightly thinner, but the hand gestures, the tilt of her head; these are achingly familiar.

He sucks in the smoke from his thin cigarette and watches for a while, soaking up the sight of her.

A small crowd has gathered, and she dispenses the poppies with enthusiasm, smiling, helping people pin them to their coats. Does she think of him as each coin clunks into her collection box? Is that why she's here, hoping she can make a difference to the ravaged minds of the living, as well as remembering the dead? The frustration of being so close gnaws at his gut and he chews at his cheek until the metallic taste of blood fills his mouth.

Many times he's dreamed of this scenario, but he's always woken with his cold hands reaching out into the dark night, longing for her warmth. Now here she is, barely thirty feet away. He closes his eyes, certain he can smell her perfume.

Two years he's been gone. Disappeared in the night because shattering lives shatters lives, and he couldn't find the way back to who he was. Things he'd seen he could just about accept, but the things he'd done he couldn't.

The apologies were wearing thin, and he knew it was only a matter of time before a near miss became a lethal blow. He left the night he woke with his hands around her neck.

She never looked at him with pity; not even when an unexpected firework sent him hurtling back to Helmand and a trail of yellow piss ran across the kitchen floor, nor when she found him shaking under the kitchen table as a police helicopter whirred above. She cradled his shaking body in her arms and shushed him like a baby. But the night she gasped for breath and pulled at his crushing hands, her eyes were lit with fear.

Now, as he watches her, he's moved to think that the likes of her could try to help the likes of him.

In his bag the last two Big Issues remain. Selling them means he'll have enough to pay for a night in the hostel. He can get a shower, wash off the stench of the street, eat a hot meal.

The cigarette sparks as he flicks it to the ground and crushes it under his boot. He turns and walks off up the High Street. He knows he'll use the money to score some shit and blast memory to oblivion. For him it's not about Remembrance, it's about an overwhelming need to forget.

Riding Solo

J E Crossman

Chantelle and Richard purchased a tandem bicycle to celebrate their first anniversary of living together. They took long weekend rides on cycling paths in and around Vancouver. Chantelle's pug, Bing, toured with them, travelling in a basket hung from the handlebars.

Chantelle likened riding tandem to making love: the exertion of bodies, panting, sweating, and a sprint to the finish. After a ride, Chantelle and Richard sometimes skipped their showers in favour of slippery, slidey lovemaking.

That was until Richard informed Chantelle that she was not the woman he wanted to ride through life with; something about being not being ready to commit and needing time to find himself.

Before Richard moved out, he said, 'I'll buy you your own bike.'

Chantelle felt sure he already had his eye on a new riding partner.

Saddled with the rent of a flat in Gastown, she took extra shifts as a server at a nearby seafood restaurant. Arriving home late one evening after a long shift, she found a unicycle parked in the hallway beside her door. A note attached to the cycle read:

Chantelle: Half a tandem bike is a unicycle. Have fun. Sorry Bing has lost his roost. R

What in the hell am I going to do with a unicycle, she thought, and what is Bing going to do without his handlebar carrier?

Chantelle slept fitfully. By morning she had a plan. The next shift, she asked Simon, one of the barmen at the restaurant with whom she connected well, whether he'd be willing to help her learn to ride the unicycle. They met that upcoming Sunday afternoon at an empty parking lot on an industrial site. She straddled the bike, put her feet on the pedals and her right arm on Simon's shoulder for balance. He put his hand on the small of her back and ran alongside her until she was able to let go. After Chantelle's successful entry into the world of unicycle riding, they went to a cafe to celebrate. Over coffee they learned more about each other and Chantelle explained how she had ended up owning a unicycle.

When time permitted, she practised riding her unicycle and, when confident, graduated to city streets. When Simon learned how much Chantelle missed Bing as a riding companion, he volunteered to teach the dog to trot ahead while she rode. Simon ran beside the unicycle with Bing on his lead and, once the dog was accustomed to the pace, Simon passed the leash to Chantelle. To celebrate the inclusion of Bing into the cycling mix, Simon treated Chantelle to ice cream that led to dinners out and then home-cooked meals at her flat. Simon rode his bicycle alongside Chantelle and Bing when his work schedule permitted.

Two months after Richard had broken off with Chantelle, she received an email from him:

Chantelle, I'm such a fool. Howz about we go biking this Sunday? R

She replied:

Sorry R, but I'm tandem again. Sure beats riding solo. Interested in swapping bikes? C

Room-mates

Angela Wooldridge

'Another one?' said Katie, hearing the giggles from upstairs.

'Two,' said Amy. 'One's in the shower.'

'In the shower? What's he been *doing* with them?'

'Oh, she's only just arrived. She works part-time at the chippy and wanted to clean up first.'

'Jeez. I always thought he was too geeky for that sort of action.'

'Some people like geeky.' Amy was picking at the dried flower arrangement on the table. 'Some people cultivate it.'

'Well, enough about that. Let's talk about you.' Katie slapped her hand away. 'What's all this crap about moving out? You can't leave me here on my own.'

More giggles floated down to them.

'It's that.' Amy jerked her head toward the stairs. 'I can't stand living in a brothel anymore.'

'Oh come on, it's not that bad.'

'He's going through the English Lit first years like a bad curry.'

'You're kidding.'

'It's a cockpit up there.'

'Don't you mean a cess-pit?'

'Oh no. I know exactly what I mean. It's his control centre of lurve. Everything's in easy reach, the switch to dim the lights, the music, the drawer with his condom selection...'

'Ew, and I left you alone in the house with him for a whole weekend last month.

'Excuse me, which one of you is Amy?'

Both girls looked up guiltily.

'Jude said you might lend me your hairdryer?' The girl in the doorway flushed at their sudden scrutiny and lifted a damp lock of hair. 'He doesn't like it when I drip on his books.'

'On his books?'

'Well of course, what did you think?' She glared at the expression on Katie's face. 'Oh, please! He's our study partner. Besides, everyone knows he's too hung up on some girl he slept with a month ago.'

Amy's fingers jerked on the papery flower pod she was holding and it split, scattering honesty seeds across the table.

(First published on Mash Stories*, 2015*)

Salt and Pepper

Margaret James

Always up for something new, is our Mavis, but this time she beat all.

At her age – that's five years older than me – and with her knees, she should be sat nicely on her sofa watching daytime television, not gadding off on all those trips with the other Evergreens, getting the coach to Whitby to go on a three day Dracula Experience or some such nonsense.

She should see sense. What if she had a fall, broke something? Who would have to pick up the pieces? Muggins, that's who.

But my sister's never been one for sitting around seeing sense. You'd think she'd always had a hole in her head on purpose to let the sense out, the way she carries on.

So anyway, off she goes to Whitby, and three days later she's back with a carrier bag and silly grin on her face that didn't bode well at all. What had she done now?

'Good time?' I ask.

'The best,' she says. 'I've brought you something, Dora,' she adds, rummaging in the bag.

'I don't want any more useless clutter. I've told you that before – there's enough dust magnets in this house already.'

'This isn't useless.'

She's still got that look on her face, the one she gets when she's done something really daft.

'You need to tell me something, don't you?' I say.

'I met this man,' she says. 'On the coach, he was on his own, like me. So we sat together, shared our chips, had a Gin and It in the hotel after dinner. He's very nice. You'll like him.'

I don't know about that, I thought.

'What's he called?' I ask. Well, you have to show some interest, don't you?

'Ted – Ted Salt,' she says. 'The people on the coach, they thought it was hilarious, seeing us two hand in hand in the Dracula Experience.' She blushes. 'So anyway, Ted says at our age you can't afford to hang around, so when we got back to the hotel we – '

'Mavis, you didn't!'

'Well, yes – we did. Then, afterwards, he said *why don't we tie the knot some day soon, make it all official*, and I said *yes*.'

'Mavis Pepper, you want your head examined.'

'I knew you'd say that. Go on, unwrap your present. Do you like it?'

'I suppose I do.'

Yes, I must admit they're quite attractive, and useful too, these little china people, Mr Salt and Mrs Pepper, both with holes in their heads.

Selfie among the Stones

Jolyon Drake

'I'm not stupid,' I said to Gareth as we neared the top of the hill. 'This wasn't really about us getting away together at all, was it? You just wanted to come up here and look at the stone circle.'

'What gave me away, Nicky?' he asked, with a smile.

This from a man with a big painting of a stone circle over his fireplace in the living room at home. From a man who would tell stories of his adventurous student days travelling the country with a friend looking for stone circles.

'I understand,' I said. 'Go and have a closer look'

I pulled my phone from my handbag and started taking photographs. First views, then the circle, and then pictures of him by the rocks.

I'm not sure how long we had been up there when the mist began to close in around us, but those sea views were quickly fading to nothing. The weather was about to turn.

'Come here, Gareth. Let's get a selfie.'

I held up my phone, trying to get an image of the pair of us with the stones in the background. Lining up the perfect shot, I was quite pleased about the mist; it made the whole thing look much moodier. He must have been pleased with it too, because as I went to press the button to take the photograph, he planted a kiss on my cheek.

And then I saw her. Standing at his shoulder.

Surprised, I turned around and then nearly dropped my phone. There was nobody there.

'What's wrong?' he asked.

I gathered my thoughts. It was a trick of the mind. There was nobody there.

'Nothing,' I said. 'It's nothing.'

'Well, take the picture then.' He put his arm around me.

I held the phone up a second time and our smiling faces again filled the screen, but then she appeared over his shoulder. Younger than us, probably in her early twenties, with long dark hair.

'Bloody hell!' he said.

I watched on the screen as he turned to face her.

'Where's she gone?' he asked, looking all around him.

'She's still there,' I said, unable to take my eyes from the screen.

'Katherine?' he said.

Katherine. There was the word that broke my heart.

I could only watch as he turned back and gazed at her image on the phone. As their eyes met. I saw her smile. Then he smiled.

'Katherine, I knew you'd be here.'

She reached out and put a hand against his face. He looked like he was leaning in towards it. I turned to look at him – and now it was like I was no longer there. I shoved the phone back into my handbag. Angry tears were already welling up.

'Give me the phone,' he said.

'I can't believe you'd bring me here!'

I walked away. There was nothing left to say. As I reached the edge of the circle he grabbed me and snatched my handbag. I stumbled and fell against a stone. Before I could do anything he had the phone in his hand, then held it in front of me.

'Unlock it,' he said.

I shook my head, tears streaming down my face. He took hold of my hand and held my thumb against the button.

'You're hurting me,' I said.

The phone unlocked at my touch, and he scrambled away, holding the phone up in front of him and frantically spinning around in circles, trying to find her.

'Katherine, it's me. I came back for you. I love you,' he shouted.

Using the stone for support I got to my feet. His voice faltered as he dropped to his knees, sobbing in the centre of the circle. I had no words of comfort to offer him as I walked into the mist, leaving him to his past.

Spoons, Guilt and Marrows

Angela Wooldridge

Billy was moving the spoon again.

Every time he found the perfect hiding place, Mum would continue her mission to spring clean the entire world, and nowhere would be safe. But this time he'd worked it out. He'd bury it in the garden. Then, when it was finally discovered in a hundred million years nobody would know it had anything to do with him or horrid old Mrs Catheter.

That was the plan anyway, until Mum followed him into the garden.

'I've got to go out, Billy. You'll have to come too.'

'But—' he made a face.

'Sorry, love, you're not old enough to be left alone.' She gave him an apologetic hug and he twisted away, conscious of the spoon in his pocket.

'Bring something to pass the time. Mrs Cathcart doesn't have much in the way of entertainment.'

Billy froze. 'Who?'

'Mrs Cathcart. The one who always goes on about her marrows.'

Billy suddenly had a cold, queasy feeling in his tummy.

Billy never meant to get into trouble. It just came looking for him.

Mum's job involved visiting people to help them fill out forms and stuff, so he always had to take something to keep himself busy.

That last time, at Mrs Catheter's, he'd had a splendid time exploring the sticky squidginess of bubble gum until it got stuck on a chair. The spoon had been lying around and scraped the gum away perfectly, but then Mum and Mrs Cath-er-whatever had returned from coo-ing over the famous marrows, so he'd shoved it in his pocket.

Later, prising off the hardened gum, he'd spotted how fancy it was and wondered if he'd accidentally stolen a family hair-piece.

Being a criminal felt horrid and he didn't want to get sent to prison, so he hid it.

'Sit here, Billy, while I help Mrs Cathcart with these forms.'

Mum set him up at the table with paper and pens, and they sat at the other end. He decided if they didn't hurry up and leave him alone, he'd have to pretend to need the loo. Old people did all sorts of odd things, so Mrs C shouldn't be too surprised to find the spoon in there.

'Thank you so much for coming over again,' she was saying to Mum. 'I'd hoped I might get some money from selling a few things and had my christening spoon ready to show to an auctioneer, but it disappeared. I was glad of the excuse not to part with it, but I do need the money.'

'I'm sure it'll turn up,' reassured Mum. 'Meanwhile let's see if we can get these benefits sorted out for you. Then you won't need to sell it.'

'You could sell your giant marrows to the circus,' suggested Billy, hoping to throw them off the scent. 'Then loads of people will visit them and you'll be a squillionaire.'

'I think you've got an inflated opinion of vegetables, young man,' said Mrs C.

'Mum says veggies are important,' he mumbled, wishing they'd take the hint and go to visit some.

He pretended to draw while he considered where to hide the spoon.

Occasionally he gave a wiggle to reassure himself it was still in his pocket.

What he hadn't bargained for was that all his wriggling would cause it to fall out, and with a humongous crash it fell to the floor.

'What was that?' asked Mum.

'Nothing. Dunno.' He scraped his foot across the floor in an attempt to locate and hide the spoon at the same time.

'Make your mind up. Is it nothing, or you don't know?' Mum eyed him suspiciously.

'Um…I dunno nothing?' he hazarded.

Mum, of course, was not fooled for a moment, and quickly found the spoon, which was nowhere near his foot.

'Billy?'

He couldn't bear the look on her face, and the story tumbled out.

Mum turned to Mrs C. 'I don't know what to say! I'm mortified!'

'I'm sorry, Mum.' Billy peered at Mrs Cathcart. 'Please don't send me to prison.'

Mrs Cathcart suddenly giggled. 'I'm sorry,' she said. 'But this takes me right back to when I was young.'

Mum blinked at her. 'Aren't you angry?'

Mrs C wiped tears from her eyes. 'I suppose I should be, with all the worry it's caused. But if young Billy hadn't taken it, I'd have sold it. So I actually owe him my thanks.'

'This is all wrong,' Mum complained. 'How's he going to learn about consequences if things turn out right?'

'I've been feeling rotten all week,' Billy reassured her. 'Worrying I'd be sent to prison and you wouldn't visit me. So if you really want,' he straightened his shoulders and turned to Mrs Cathcart. 'I'll go and look at your marrows.'

Stitched Up

Dianne Bown-Wilson

Her face was exquisite but what enthralled me were her fingers, moving like pistons, morphing grey needles and white wool into a blur.

When I'd walked into the dentist's waiting room she was already there, small, slender, probably mid-thirties – my age. As the reception desk was next door the two of us were alone, so I positioned myself a few seats away, facing her, and reached for a magazine. As I did, she smiled, revealing perfect white teeth – perhaps she spent a lot of time here? – and my eyes locked into her mesmerising gaze.

Disconcerted, I switched my focus to her hands. 'Very impressive - what are you making?'

'You'll laugh when I tell you.'

'Oh?'

'It's a wedding cake.'

'No kidding – you're knitting *a wedding cake*?'

'Yep. I'm just glad I'm not knitting the dress, though I have, on several occasions.'

'I'm gobsmacked.'

She shrugged. 'It's amazing what people want. What used to be a hobby is now my job. I even write books about it.'

Throughout our exchange, her hands never faltered; it was as if they were attached to someone else.

'Nice work…'

'Carrie Grey?' The sudden appearance of the dentist prevented any further exchange. She stood up, pushed the knitting into her bag and smiled at me. 'Good to meet you.'

'Yeah. Take care.'

My last glimpse was of the back of her head, blonde hair twisted up like yarn.

Following my appointment, I went straight to a bookshop. Three titles with her name on proved she had been telling the truth. A sensation as insistent as an itch made me want to own some link to her, so I decided to buy *How to Knit Knickknacks*. The sales assistant shot me an odd look.

Once home, I tracked down her website. She posed with the air of a sorceress amongst knitted animals, food, plants, flowers, footwear and clothes. When I clicked on a video link, it seemed she spoke to me directly: '*Whatever a heart desires I can create. Nothing is too bizarre.*'

I held out for three weeks before I let myself go to her house. Hours of online detective work encouraged me to think she was single; I'd brought flowers hoping I wasn't wrong. I rang the bell, mouth dry but palms clammy, and within seconds she opened the door smiling as if she'd known I would come.

'You remember me?'

'Of course.'

I thrust the blooms at her. 'I couldn't stop thinking about your knitting – it's magical somehow.'

'So people say.'

'May I come in?'

'If you're sure.' I had no chance to reflect on her meaning as I followed her down the hallway to a closed door. She paused, then pushed it open.

Reclining on a sofa was a full-size, knitted replica of me – glasses, dark curly hair, my quite large nose – dressed exactly as I'd been the day we met.

I must have gasped; she laughed.

Her eyes flickered like a snake tongue. 'Whatever a heart desires…'

(First published in Writing Magazine*, April 2018)*

Tapestry

Su Bristow

This is my favourite tree. The palms are scaly; they hurt your hands and tear your clothes, but this one has smooth bark and good branches. Other people have climbed it before, I can tell, but today there's only me. I go higher than I've ever been, so high that I can feel the tree moving in the wind, trying to push its roots through the earth and wade away downriver. Maybe it really is walking, very slowly, so when I'm old and my granddaughter climbs here, she'll see a different view.

This high, I can see forever, right into the desert where the trees stop. I can see the boys at school under the neem tree, reciting scripture; there's my brother Latif, watching the birds and daydreaming again. There's my mother washing clothes in the river; she straightens up, shades her eyes and calls, and a little bit later my name floats up like a startled bird and flies away on the breeze: 'Habiba!'

I hug my tree and bite my arm. Bad girl, not to answer; but if I did, those boys smoking in the bushes would hear me, and the girls drying herbs in the sun would know the boys are watching them. That dog skulking there in the reeds would see me and scamper away, and the birds feeding in the palms would take flight.

I'm a secret-keeper, up here. Life can only go on if I let it. If I call out, Mahmoud's father will have to beat him for smoking, and Hana's big sister, pressed against a tree with the arms of a boy around her, will be sent away in disgrace and not have to marry the shopkeeper Iqbal, who is her father's friend. Good girl, to keep quiet, to know things and never say. I press my cheek to the bark and whisper, so only my tree can hear. 'Sharif has run away to join the rebels. He says the soldiers are coming.'

My tree walks slowly on.

The Blacksmith's Arms

Angela Wooldridge

'Love spells,' complained Olwyn, as she flipped through her spell book. 'Why can't people be more imaginative?'

Still, business was business, so she gathered the ingredients. Except for…

'Three hairs from the head of the person desired. Huh,' she remarked to the cat, who dozed by the stove and completely ignored her. 'I should've told Melinda to get those herself, the amount I'm charging. Although…' She'd have to track Melinda down and explain, then trust her to get it right. 'No,' she decided. 'Not when I'm seeing Jonas later anyway.'

If Melinda had to choose an object of love, then Jonas the blacksmith was a good specimen, Olwyn mused later that day. She'd arrived at the smithy for the final stages of the ale they'd been brewing together for the village fayre.

As they stirred and measured, she watched him from the corner of her eye, admiring the play of muscles beneath his skin, the glow of the fire reflected in his eyes.

'What's wrong?' He ran a hand across his face and checked it. 'Have I got something on my nose?'

She laughed and shook her head. It was a shame; Jonas would be wasted on Melinda.

'Here,' he dipped out a tankard each and passed one to her. 'Careful though, in case I've put something in there to make you fall in love with me.' He winked.

'Witches can't fall in love,' she said, and matched him drink for drink.

She woke in the pale light of dawn to an unfamiliar bedroom, a heavy arm about her waist and a contented sigh in her ear.

Oh, what have I done? she mourned. You could never be for me!

'Best we pretend this never happened,' she whispered to his sleeping form. She snipped the required hairs from his head, but couldn't resist pressing a last kiss against his lips before she slipped away.

What have I done? She refused to watch Melinda leave, potion in hand. Instead she leaned against the door and kicked it until her toes hurt.

'Witches can't fall in love,' she reminded herself.

A hammering at the door roused her from her self-pity.

'Don't cry,' said Jonas when he saw her reddened eyes. 'I told her it wouldn't work.' He tossed Melinda's bottle onto the table.

'Witches don't cry,' she said automatically. Then, 'What do you mean?'

'I told Melinda that there was no point in trying as I already love another.' He wiped a tear from her cheek and held it up to show her. 'Does this mean you're not a witch anymore?'

He loved someone else? She gazed numbly at the teardrop. 'I suppose not.'

'Then come live with me,' he urged. 'We brew a mean pint together; I've a fancy to open a tavern.' He smiled down at her, 'We'll call it *The Blacksmith's Arms*.'

The Blue Bench

Su Bristow

'Here I am,' he said. 'Again. I hope you can hear me, but I guess it doesn't matter really. I – oops, this seat's on its last legs.' He shifted further along, away from the arm of the bench that was leaning out at a dangerous angle. 'Will it still work if the bench isn't here any more? Maybe I should try to mend it somehow; what do you think? You know I'm no good with my hands, you told me so often enough.'

The woman smiled, and reached out a hand to touch his cheek, though of course he couldn't feel it. In fact, his sudden move meant they were overlapping a little, and that felt somehow improper. She slid along to the far end of the bench, gleaming with new paint and black enamel. Bright blue, she'd chosen. 'Stupid colour for a garden seat,' he'd said at the time, before skulking off to be somewhere –

80

anywhere – else than here. She'd painted it herself. There was still paint under her fingernails.

'When it's gone, it's gone,' she said. 'Maybe there'll be another bench, maybe not. I'll still be here when you come, don't worry.'

He sat as though listening, head on one side, the way he used to as a child, stopping halfway through his cornflakes to consider a new idea. 'Why isn't the sky green? Does it go all the way to heaven?' But maybe he was just listening to the wind in the poplars, grown tall and unkempt since her day.

'I miss you still,' he said. 'You know that, don't you? You went too soon for me.'

She sighed. 'Why do you think I'm still here? It's been ten years now; to the day. I see you've brought freesias again. But all in all, you're not doing too badly. I did like other flowers too, you know.' But he really wasn't listening; he started to speak before she'd finished.

'The thing is, the thing I wanted to tell you today,' he said, and his fingers picked at the flowers as he spoke, shredding the delicate petals. 'I've met someone, someone special. We've been going out for a while now, and – well, we're going to move in together.'

She waited, very still.

'I've told her all about you,' he said, talking very fast now. His fingers had moved on, prising up flakes of paint from the slats of the bench. She raised her hand to stop him, and checked herself, and smiled.

'And what she said was, well, what she thinks is that it's time for me to move on, to let go.' He finished, breathless.

'Sensible girl,' she said, but low, as if to herself. He didn't hear her anyway.

'So I won't be coming again for a while. I really want to make this work, you know? And that's one thing you taught me, that you can't expect things to just work, without making an effort. I've never forgotten what you said to me that day.'

'Ah,' she said, 'but if I'd known they were my last words, I'd have said something much more trivial.'

It was no use. '"You get back what you put in," you said, and I slammed the door in your face and never saw you again. I'd give anything to be able to do it differently now. You know that, don't you?'

She stood up. 'Time to go, I think. Now that it's not true any more.' She touched his hair, briefly, and maybe he did feel something after all; he put his hand up and their fingers met.

She turned away.

The Caretaker

Clare Girvan

The trees are tall in the overgrown and sunny garden where birds sing during the day and urban foxes bark at night. A little sunlight comes through the glass in the morning, perhaps, but the rooms are twilit with green leaves. Lamps make cosy pools of light.

'I need lots of light,' says one tenant. 'I get depressed.'

'Not here,' says Mr Neville. 'You'll see.'

Despite the gloom, they see, and take comfort in the shadows.

Mr Neville cleans the rooms of number 76 Woodstock Road when the tenants leave. He takes out the rubbish, dusts the woodwork, checks the electricity, replaces everything as he likes it. The tenants always move the furniture, but when they have gone, he puts it all back where it should be. He works slowly and lovingly, with method.

Sometimes the rooms are left clean, sometimes not. He doesn't mind much either way, but on the whole, he prefers his lady tenants. They generally keep things tidy and take their bits and pieces with them when they go. He likes to think of them living out their lives in the tiny rooms at the top of the stairs, cooking in the cramped kitchens.

Surroundings are a matter of indifference to most of the men, cleaning an afterthought, if done at all, bottles left under the bed. Mr Neville is tolerant, only mildly reprimanding when he comes for the rent and they argue.

Failing human beings come to his door for rest and comforting. A cup of tea, a chat, offered at the exact moment. He never asks what brings them or how they know about the house, but he lets them in. Down the years they have come, with the arrival of the railway, the motor car, the aeroplane, the computer. One by one, the unknown, the might-be-known, a poet, a painter, a battered suffragette, the sorrowful of the world. They are all there because they need love. Mr Neville knows. He has always known.

'I'm just the caretaker,' he says. 'I take care of things.'

The house soaks up their lives. Their happiness and sadness seep into the walls and become part of them. And as the house absorbs all that has made them, they grow new skins and emerge into the light.

'Notice is hereby given...'

It's the end of the line for Mr Neville. Woodstock Road is to be demolished to make way for a housing estate.

'What about my residents?' he asks. 'Where are they supposed to go?'

'It's a compulsory purchase order,' the man says. 'Alternative accommodation will be offered.'

'And if we don't want it?'

'I'm sorry.' Another way of saying, 'Tough.'

What use is a caretaker with nothing to take care of? He tidies the garden, takes leave of each plant. He knows their everyday names and their Sunday best. They will die and he grieves for them.

The house is only an empty casing, everything gone, down to the last little bit of soap in a white bathroom. He locks the door, stands on the closely-mown front lawn, picks a rose and sticks it in his buttonhole, then sets off down the road. He will find another.

The Night Visitors

Clare Girvan

The cat, skinny, bedraggled and sad-eyed, came out of the wood to her cottage and mewled at her door.

'You poor thing,' she said. 'Are you hungry?' She opened a tin of sardines and it ate ravenously, then curled up and slept on the sofa all night. In the morning it was gone, but it returned the following night with two more skinny, bedraggled cats with sad eyes. She opened two tins of tuna. They ate ravenously then slept on the sofa, curled round each other like conjoined Chelsea buns. In the morning all three were gone.

The next night a dozen skinny, bedraggled cats with sad eyes came out of the wood and mewled at her door. She took mince from the freezer and they ate ravenously, then curled up on the sofa in a furry heap. In the morning they were gone. The next night there was a circle of thirty skinny, bedraggled cats with sad eyes at her door.

'No,' she said. 'No more. I can't afford you all.'

The cats gazed at her with sad eyes and mewled.

'No,' she said. 'There isn't any more.'

The silent circle advanced, backing her into the house. There was always more.

The Silver Spoon

Cherry Gilchrist

Here's the spoon Auntie Bee used to dole out the
jam. My little sister and I couldn't be trusted to help
ourselves moderately. What was it she'd recite?
Something about: 'Bury me late, bury me soon, bury
me with a silver spoon…'

Then, 'Waste not, want not,' she'd chirrup,
spreading every drop of jam across the bread. She
had a saying for everything.

Uncle Arthur didn't like waste either. Or
anyone touching his precious collection of ticking
clocks. Auntie Bee had to wind them at exactly the
right moment. 'Pride and joy, pride and joy,' she
mused as she dusted them.

One day, she looked different, all bruised
around her eye.

'What happened to your face, Auntie?'

'Least said, soonest mended. Wouldn't hurt a fly. Flies don't know their own strength.'

My mother stored Auntie Bee's things when she finally had to go into a home. Now Mum's moving into a retirement flat, so here I am, sifting through them.

Ah! A china egg cup, in the shape of a hen. That glossy dip in her back, that golden beak.

'Heckety Peckety my black hen, she lays eggs for gentlemen,' carolled Auntie Bee, dishing out our tea. There were two eggcups, but now there's only one – I can still hear the shouting as Uncle Arthur smashed the other against the wall.

And then Uncle Arthur lay dribbling in his chair. 'He's had a stroke,' said Auntie Bee. But wasn't a stroke something nice?

'Bury me late, bury me soon…' she recited, giving him his medicine on her prized silver spoon. 'It's sweet,' she said, 'a real treat for him.'

Mum told us Uncle Arthur had died. 'Probably a blessing.'

I rub the silver spoon on my jumper. Tomorrow I'll dig it into the earth of her grave. 'Rest in peace, Auntie Bee.'

The Writing Retreat

Cathie Hartigan

Sunday

Arrived! Journey arduous, but hey, aren't retreats supposed to be miles from anywhere? Villa is fantastic! Weather perfect! Blue and hazy with heat. My room is huge, and I've a view out the window, over valley, between mountains, all the way to the sea. The sea! Tuscany, I love you, although I hope there are no scorpions in the shower, a trenchant memory from 1989. I will be calm.

Monday

Everyone's arrived now. Eight of us altogether. Tamsin can't be twenty, the rest of us are clearly over fifty: six women and Jasper, not yet seen without his mirrored shades. I can't tell where he's looking although can hazard a guess. No wifi, and signal weak even when standing on chair in utility room.

Enormous shield bugs, each a mini Thunderbirds 2, fly mostly into things. They drop and lie upturned, legs whirling. Glittery lizards dart into nearest bush when disturbed. The air is drenched with the scent of geranium and thyme. I think I will write a poem.

Tuesday

Woke up to owls in night and gunfire in morning. It's hunting season. Jubilant barking from forest accompanies breakfast conversation. So much for intros and backstories, we all bond condemning whole bloody business. Rather afraid to go out. Shield bugs also called stink bugs apparently. Tiresome today, one dropped into Jasper's dinner. He didn't notice (I blame the shades) but was grateful when I pointed it out.

Wednesday

Blue-green and shadowed grey, shoulders of forested mountains snooze. The poem is coming on. Others are beavering away. Except Tamsin. Clearly, she's come on a swimming retreat. Jasper hasn't written anything either. Says he meditates more these days. Who knew that spot beside the pool could be so spiritually uplifting?

Found out how stink bugs got their name when accidentally trod on one. Squelchy and malodorous mess. Yuck. Mouse under sofa makes me jump. No spiders though, or scorpions, thank goodness.

Thursday

Shooting again this morning, even though mist means a blank beyond edge of terrace. Spooky! Perhaps hunters will shoot each other? We all giggle, and follow up with tales of retribution, cruel and true.

Bugs are a pain. Maybe damp brought them in, as many more in house now. They come in through rotting window frames. Whirl about like clockwork toys. At least they're slow. Saw mouse in kitchen; gone in a flash. Supper's black rice tastes good, but really does resemble droppings. Afterwards I read out one verse of stalled poem to polite grunts. Drink two big glasses of wine. Bugs have hidden in nightie and fall on head like conkers. Whack with slippers and go to bed with lavender bag held to nose.

Friday

Sleepless night. Palpitations, indigestion (perhaps they *were* droppings) and owls in relentless screech/hoot debate *extremely* close to house. Woke to rain, commotion and attack from swarm, no, absolute *plague* of bugs, hurling themselves at windows, doors, up drainpipes, through vents, every gap in every possible place. Now in our beds, our clothes, the stove, bugs are toast, the printer coughs bloodied paper. Close combat required. Our weapons: only kitchen roll and broom, but we are ruthless. Tamsin, long-legged and youthful, the joyous assassin of high places: lintels, ceiling beams, tops of wardrobes. Jasper is useless, but reveals he's waiting for cataract ops, so is forgiven. A frenzy of death until nothing is left but a reeking miasma, despite bin bags tightly knotted. We put them outside.

Saturday

Last whole day. Bugs vanished from Earth's face. Swept away on brisk breeze? View to sea. Azure sky. Hands of rusty fig leaves splayed all over ground. Poem remembered but feels too late for resurrection. Final dinner and mutual appreciation session. Is group glue stronger for killing spree? Seems so, but all too sheepish to say.

Sunday

Woke to gentle pop of hunter's gun, with warmth on cheek from late October sun – oh wait! Perhaps creativity and poem not dead after all. Quickly write down flash of inspiration. Tidy up later as now time to leave. All sad. *Arrivederci* Tuscany. Back next year?

Things Mr Google Doesn't Know

Dianne Bown-Wilson

It's snowing today. If you were here, studying the flakes fluttering down from the mud grey sky, you'd be full of questions: *Why's snow white, Gramma? What's the biggest snowman ever built? Why do we only get snow sometimes?*

All kids are inquisitive, but you…Since you first learned to speak, your hunger for knowledge has been insatiable. Your Dad joked that you shot into the world asking *why?* – but everyone pretended they hadn't heard because they didn't know the answer.

Despite all your questions, I love talking to you, relishing the freedom of never having to worry if I'm saying the right thing in the most diplomatic way. It's how conversations should be.

'The older you get, the more careful you have to be,' I said once, unintentionally thinking out loud. We were walking; I remember your warm little paw in mine.

You frowned, 'Why?'

'Oh, because people are looking for signs that you're getting forgetful or cantankerous and if they think you are, they're all poised ready to lock you away.'

Your eyes welled up. 'I won't let them lock you away – ever!'

I laughed and picked you up, swinging you round to swirl away your fears.

When I put you down, you looked up at me, solemn again. 'Gramma, what does *cantankerous* mean?'

I think you were only four then, not a grown-up six, like now. When your Dad was your age, he asked lots of questions too. But these days, now we can access all the world's knowledge online, coming up with answers is much easier.

I always thought it important that whatever you asked, I should answer factually. But as your questions became more complex my immediate response often had to be, 'I don't know, Petey, but I know a man who does: I'll ask Mr Google.'

Mr Google, as we discovered, knows *everything* about *everything*, although, sometimes, translating all his knowledge into something you'd understand and find interesting took me hours of reading and clicking through. But I enjoyed the challenge, still do, though these days the few questions I research on my own behalf aren't nearly as fascinating as yours.

And sadly, just lately I've discovered that actually, he doesn't know it all.

Six months ago, your Mum and Dad split up, and she's taken you with her to her parents' place which is over two hundred miles away. On top of that, apparently she's decided that she doesn't want you to see me now although your Dad says that you still want to. But it seems you don't get to see him often, either…

That Skype call yesterday when you were at his place, the first time we'd spoken for ages, near enough broke my heart. We both tried to be brave, didn't we? – laughing and joking – but then you had to ask that question: 'Gramma, when will I see you again?'

Fighting back tears I could only say, 'I don't know, sweetheart.' There was no point adding, *but we could ask Mr Google.*

Wedding List

Sophie Duffy

White linen tablecloth. Stained with Lamb Bhuna on their first anniversary.

Four slice toaster. Four years of breakfasts. Crumb drawer catches fire.

Kettle. Tea, coffee, hot chocolate, Bovril. Aunts, colleagues, builders, neighbours, mothers-in-law, and a so-called friend who drained more than she could know. Replaced five times. And the kettle.

Dinner service. Six settings. One cup chipped. A cracked saucer for the cat who ran off with the neighbour. A plate of spaghetti hurled and spattered against the kitchen wall.

Portmeirion cake stand and silver-plated knife. Too much for Betty Crocker's efforts.

Cut-glass decanter. An unopened box in the cupboard under the stairs – no need to decant lager.

Napkin rings. A spontaneous game of quoits on her 30th. Her aim was true.

Canteen of cutlery. Stainless steel. Sheffield. Their last holiday before.

Meat thermometer and turkey baster. One child.

Ice bucket. Useful for bumps and bruises.

Champagne flutes. Another child. His aim was true.

Muffin tins. Muffin tops.

Bread machine. Shelved accusingly in the garage.

Pyrex jug. A sunny summer evening. Sangria with her old college friends. Hangover from hell.

Saucepans. Rice. Pasta. Spuds. Veg. Custard. Baked beans. Spuds. Boil-in-the-bag lamb shanks from Aldi. Spuds. Spuds.

Towel bale. Turquoise. Now grey. Useful for mopping up.

Poacher. Broken eggshells. Walking on eggshells.

Pressure cooker.

Alarm clock.

Dutch oven. The gift that keeps on giving.

A sheaf of paper. A signature.

A broom to sweep under the carpets.

Sheets. Clean.

About the Authors

You can find out more about our authors on the
Exeter Writers website: www.exeterwriters.org.uk.

Printed in Great Britain
by Amazon